2011   B292286876

P9-CQA-927

WITHDRAWN

Orchards

Orchards

Holly Thompson

ILLUSTRATIONS BY GRADY MCFERRIN

DELACORTE PRESS

Text copyright © 2011 by Holly Thompson
Jacket photograph copyright © 2011 by Jean Fan
Illustrations copyright © 2011 by Grady McFerrin
All rights reserved. Published in the United States by Delacorte Press,
an imprint of Random House Children's Books, a division of
Random House, Inc., New York.
Delacorte Press is a registered trademark and the colophon
is a trademark of Random House, Inc.
Visit us on the Web! www.randomhouse.com/teens
Educators and librarians, for a variety of teaching tools,
visit us at www.randomhouse.com/teachers
Library of Congress Cataloging-in-Publication Data
Thompson, Holly.
Orchards / Holly Thompson. — 1st ed.
p. cm.
Summary: Sent to Japan for the summer after an eighth-grade classmate's
suicide, half-Japanese, half-Jewish Kana Goldberg tries to fit in with
relatives she barely knows and reflects on the guilt she feels over the
tragedy back home.
ISBN 978-0-385-73977-1 (hc : alk. paper) — ISBN 978-0-375-89834-1 (ebook)
— ISBN 978-0-385-90806-1 (glb : alk. paper)
[1. Novels in verse. 2. Suicide—Fiction. 3. Racially mixed people—Fiction.
4. Japan—Fiction.] I. Title.
PZ7.5.T45Or 2011
[Fic]—dc22
2010023724
The text of this book is set in 11-point Cochin.
Book design by Marci Senders
Printed in the United States of America
10 9 8 7 6 5 4 3 2 1
First Edition

In memory of Julie, David and Makiko, and dedicated to survivors everywhere

Chapter 1
Because of You

One week after
you stuffed a coil of rope
into your backpack
and walked uphill into
Osgoods' orchard
where blooms were still closed fists

my father looked up
summer airfares
to Tokyo

why?
I protested
it wasn't my fault
I didn't do anything!

exactly!
my mother hissed
and made the call
to her older sister
my aunt
in Shizuoka

nothing would change
their minds

all my mother
would say
as I followed her
through garden beds
transplanting cubes of seedlings
she'd grown under lights
in hothouses

all she'd say
row after row
in tight-lipped
talk-down
do-as-I-say
Japanese
was
you can reflect
in the presence of your ancestors

not that I'm alone
in being sent away—
Lisa's off to summer school
Becca to Bible camp
Mona to cousins in Quebec
Emily to help in her uncle's store
Erin to math camp
Abby to some adventure program
Noelle to her father's
Gina to her mother's
Namita to New Jersey . . .
all twenty-nine
eighth-grade girls
scattered, as Gina said,
like beads
from a necklace
snapped

but we weren't a necklace
strung in a circle
we were more
an atom:
electrons
arranged in shells
around Lisa,
Becca and Mona
first shell solid,
the rest of us
in orbitals farther out
less bound
less stable
and you—
in the least stable
most vulnerable
outermost shell

you sometimes
hovered near
sometimes drifted off
some days were hurled far
from Lisa
our nucleus
whose biting wit made us
laugh
      spin
           revolve
around her
always close to her
indifferent to orbits
like yours
farther out than
ours

after you were
found in the grove
of Macs and Cortlands
that were still tight fists
of not-yet-bloom
and the note was found
on your dresser
by your mother
who brought it to the principal
who shared it with police
who called for an investigation
and pulled in counselors
from all over the district

word got around

and people in town
began to stare
and talk
and text
about our uncaring
generation

still
I don't think I
personally
did anything to drive you
to perfect slipknots
or learn to tie a noose . . .
with what?
I wonder
shoelaces?
backpack cords?
drawstrings in your gym shorts
as you waited for your turn
at the softball bat?

because of you, Ruth,
I'm exiled
to my maternal grandmother, Baachan,
to the ancestors at the altar
and to Uncle, Aunt and cousins
I haven't seen in three years —
not since our last trip back
for Jiichan's funeral
when Baachan
told my sister Emi
she was just right
but told me
I was fat
should eat
less
fill myself eighty percent
no more
each meal

but then I was small
then I didn't have hips
then was before this bottom
inherited from my father's
Russian Jewish mother

my mother was
youngest
of four children born
to my grandparents
mikan orange farmers
in a Shizuoka village of sixty households
where eldest son
inherits all

but there were
no sons
in her generation
so my aunt
eldest daughter
took in a husband who
took on the Mano name
took over the Mano holdings
became sole heir
head of household
my uncle

into my suitcase
my mother has stuffed
gifts—
socks
dish towels
framed photos of Emi and me
last year's raspberry jam
pancake mix
maple syrup—
and ten books for me to finish
by September

books she didn't pick
I know
because she only reads novels
in Japanese
and these ten are
in English—
books chosen by a librarian
or teacher
or other mother
with themes of
       responsibility
       self-discovery
       coming-of-age
       reaching out
I GET IT
I want to shout

she also changed dollars
into yen
and divided bills
into three envelopes
labeled in Japanese —
one for spending
one for transportation and school fees
one with gift money for Buddhist ceremonies
to honor her father — my Jiichan,
this third summer
since the year
of his passing

the nonstop flight to Narita
is thirteen hours
but
door to door
my home in New York
to theirs in Shizuoka
is a full twenty-four

on the plane there is
time . . .
for movies
books
journal entries
meals
magazines
movies
sleep
meals
magazines
sleep
boredom
apprehension

I have never been to
Japan alone
never traveled anywhere alone
except sleepovers
and overnight camp
for a week in Vermont

on the plane
flight attendants chat with me
unaccompanied minor
praise my language abilities
assume it's a
happy occasion
my returning
to the village of my mother's childhood
for the summer

but they don't know
what I know, Ruth—
that it's all
because of you

Chapter 2
Half

Before landing
I'm bumped up
to business
to a seat of vast slippery leather
with ample room even for my
Russian Jewish bottom
that Baachan will scorn
but it's on the aisle
so I can't see out to
       coast
       fields
       towns
       cities
whatever is out there
where I will soon be

after landing
and immigration
and baggage claim
and customs
my older cousins
Koichi and Yurie
appear with a banner
that says *Kana-chan*
take my bags
bow to airline staff
and lead me to a parking lot and van

following them
I see they are both
lean
Yurie's legs two
skinny
sticks
below
a hipless
butt

on the highway
we drive past wet paddies
with green lines of rice
forests of bamboo and cedar
trees different from in New York
tile-roofed houses
town centers
then offices
apartments
housing complexes
cities of concrete
buildings all jammed close
like the play blocks
of the Collins kid I sit for

will Emi sit for him
instead
this summer?

thinking of him
thinking of her
thinking of home
I'm homesick already
I think

from the front
passenger seat
Yurie says
you'll live with me in my room

I thank her and add
words my mother
would want me to say—
I'm sorry to be
a bother

no bother
she says
I work during the day
so I'm mostly not there

she says she hopes
I will have enough privacy
she hopes
I will feel at ease
she says she is sorry
about what happened but that
she is glad
I am here
that it will be
like having
a sister

as we hum along the highway
Koichi puts on music
and I fall asleep
dream an earthquake sways
our New York house
bends and flexes it
like a bamboo frond
till Emi's and my second-story room
bows down
down
nearly scrapes
the ground
and I jerk
awake

Kohama Village is dark
when we arrive
cross the narrow bridge over the river
and veer left at the village hall
where I learned to ride a unicycle
taking turns with Emi
when the adults were all
at Jiichan's cremation
three years ago

Koichi wedges the van
into the driveway
cuts the engine

figures appear
in the still night

Baachan looks me over in yard light
as I step from the van
and straighten
she notes my size
and grunts
Aunt bows,
takes my two hands
firm in hers, says
okaerinasai—welcome back
Uncle nods and nods
I bow and bow
Koichi unloads my bags
Yurie hooks her arm in mine
and leads me inside
to their home
my home
for now

after I wash my hands
twice
and gargle
as instructed
I join them in the front room
where Baachan kneels
before the altar
tells Jiichan
I'm here
tells the ancestors
I'm here
announces my visit
yanks me down to kneel
light incense
close my eyes
and reflect
I suppose

later, Aunt takes the jar of my mother's jam
that I'd pulled from my suitcase
and places it beside altar greens
and incense
as an offering
to Jiichan

the first three days
in Kohama
I wake up
early
even before Yurie
who rises at five
to dress
and wash
and start the laundry
and help Baachan
make the miso soup
serve the rice and fish
and eat and drive to her job at a pharmacy

I try to help
but my ears
aren't used
to Baachan's words
Aunt and Uncle and Koichi's words
so much Japanese
so fast and constant
not
the half-and-half mix
of English
and Japanese
I hear from my family
or the Japlish I share
with Emi
in New York

to my relatives here
I am Kana-*chan*
I am Japanese
period
even though it should be a
semicolon
since half of me
is not Japanese
even though I'm
Kanako Goldberg
and feel alien here

I try to learn fast
make up for my
non-Japanese half
but Uncle makes
remarks
like after I set the breakfast table —
how are we supposed to eat . . .
with our hands?

I rush to set out chopsticks . . .
seconds
too late

they seem to think
I can just switch
one half of me
on
and leave the other
half of me
off
but I'm like
warm water
pouring from a faucet
the hot
and cold
both flowing
as one

Chapter 3
Uniform

But even being away
from home
even trying to be
all Japanese
is easy
a million times easier
than the hardest thing
I've ever done, Ruth,
which was to speak to your mother
during shiva
to utter the Hebrew words
of consolation my father taught me
which seemed
no consolation
to her

your father, your brother
neighbors, relatives
your dogs even
side by side, alert, waiting —
for you?

everyone gathered
in the house
I'd never been inside

that was when I wondered
had my mother converted
to Judaism
had my family gone
to synagogue
had I attended
Hebrew school
had I been at
your Bat Mitzvah
like Sarah, before she moved away,
would it have been
different?

but my father always said that when he married my mother
he never intended to make
a Japanese woman
Jewish

farm rhythm means
meals at six, twelve and six
setting out soy sauce
            bulbs of sweet-sour *rakkyo*
            pickled daikon
            salted plums
dishing out rice
ladling soup
bowed heads to begin
slurping
chewing
light talk
clearing
tea

no dessert

I wish Yurie didn't have to work
I wish she could be here all day
I wish Emi
were here

Aunt takes me on errands the second day
Baachan sends me alone the third—
on foot
        to tofu shop
        and green grocer
on a bicycle with basket
        to fish shop
        hardware store
        and district library
        three villages away
where I linger
gaze at rows of spines
in Japanese
and a few old picture books
and textbooks
in English

I get a card
to borrow
manga biographies
of chemists and physicists
and an English high school text
Physics and You

because
thanks to you, Ruth,
I can't seem to read the books
my mother sent with me
can't get past first pages
can't handle building plots
or tolerate conflict
the unpredictability of fiction

I can only stomach
Marie Curie
Albert Einstein
and *Physics and You* —
facts
numbers
equations
velocity and relative motion
kinetic energy
rotation
acceleration
gravity
inertia

on the last day
of the fourth week in June
my fourth day in Kohama
still jet-lagged
groggy and just starting
to get the hang
of Baachan's Japanese
Uncle takes me
to meet the principal
and homeroom teacher
at the district middle school
on a finger of land that pokes into the bay
where they've arranged for me
to attend classes
part-time
for four weeks

the school sits atop a hill
of *mikan* terraces
and a steep slope of forest
where egrets roost—

the white of the birds
flowers
I'd thought
from afar

after that
each weekday morning
I join two other girls
from Kohama
cycling the road
along the still-calm bay
to that finger of land
and pedal
up
up
and up
an impossible hill
till I'm soaked
pushing the bike
wearing a second cousin's uniform
that Aunt enlarged

sailor top over
navy pleated skirt

when I'm dressed in it
Uncle says
NOW you look
Japanese

Chapter 4
Orbiting

School is not my idea of summer
but in this Shizuoka middle school
early July
is still first term
with three weeks left
till summer break
when all my days will be spent
in the family *mikan* groves

now in classes I sweat
     everywhere
          armpits
          neck
          back
          knees
          even eyelids
as I try to follow lessons
take notes, mark textbooks —
grateful
for the first time ever
for all those years of Saturdays
my mother made me
attend Japanese weekend school
in New York

watching groups of students
those left out
those harassed
those orbiting in unstable outer circles
I think of you, us
and how we all were
and I just want to know, Ruth—

when you started talking
to Jake Osgood
who Lisa liked
who Lisa hoped to go out with
who Lisa had enlisted all of our help
all winter
to get

when you and Jake
just sat down on the
sidewalk and
leaned back against the school wall
    and laughed
    and shrugged
    and just talked casual
        like you were best friends—

what did you expect?

if you had told me
what you had told Jake
if Jake had told Lisa
what you'd told him
if you had told Jake
what to tell Lisa
if Lisa had told us
I want to think
the texts and chat
would have ended and we
would have listened
would have understood

even though
not one of us
eighth-grade girls
had ever heard
of your condition

only Jake
with his oldest sister
in
and out
of hospitals
correctly read
your highs
and lows

here as a guest third-year student
at this middle school
I'm an oddity
foreigner
Japanese
but not Japanese
the first half or double
most have ever met

they ask me
do I have dual citizenship?
do I write *kanji*?
were my eyes ever blue?
why's my hair so dark?
do I eat bread three times a day?
they giggle scraps of conversation in English
explain things loud and slow in Japanese
until I realize I have to stop being shy
babble back
in Japanese slang
set them straight that
bilingual means
bilingual
period

Chapter 5
Thinning

Middays at school
after eating the *bento* lunch
that Baachan packs for me—
never-enough-rice with
tiny morsels of lightly seasoned fish
or hardly-any-meat
beside an undressed salad
plus a boiled quail's egg
and pickled vegetables
and a mini-taste-of-fruit in
a perfect balance of five colors
feast for the eyes but not my stomach—
I cycle back along curves of coast
to Kohama

I sip chilled tea
in the kitchen
change in Yurie's room
and snack
from a supply
hidden
in an inner zip section
of my suitcase

peanuts with nori-covered rice crackers
"salad"-flavored pretzel sticks
squares of green-tea chocolate
miniature castellas
and tiny individually wrapped
pancakes
filled with
sweet
velvety
azuki

then I lie by the fan
and sneak a listen —
my mother having banned
        music players
        big earrings
        makeup
from my luggage —
she doesn't know that Emi, faithful sister
shoved in my iPod
last minute

I listen in the afternoons
before *mikan* work
or helping Baachan weed
or Aunt shop

and sometimes at night —
deep middle of night —
when Yurie sleeps heavily and I
lie alive
alone
thinking
of you

thinking that
dipolar I know—
two poles
earth's north and south
every magnet has two poles
like poles repel
magnetic poles are near
        not at
the geographic poles—
these things I know

but not bipolar
the disorder
that can drive people to do
what you did

after my listen
I ride the truck up with Koichi to
whichever hillside grove they are working
that day

we blast the radio
and if I like the song
or he likes the song
Koichi drives slow
sometimes stalling out
halfway up the hill
if we reach the grove too soon
we wait for the song to end
and change to another song
before turning off the engine
to join Aunt and Uncle
thinning excess fruit
from the trees

Uncle gives me cotton gloves
and shows me how to thin clusters of
cherry-size *mikan*
that I pick and let drop

hard and green
they crunch underfoot

I learn to leave
only five of the best
to mature

as Aunt, Uncle, Koichi and I
work a row of trees
sometimes we talk
and Aunt asks about
my classes
in Japan
my classes
in New York
my home in New York
my mother's business
my sister's love of running
even my father's work in
county court

but not about
you

I know they know
about you and I know
they know I was one of those
labeled *at risk*
referred for further counseling
and sessions where
time and again
I was asked
how are you feeling?
are you sleeping?
what are you thinking?

there I tried to talk
there counselors listened

but here in Kohama
no one seems to know
how to talk
about you

including me

I start to grow more used
to the work
the endless stretch of time
in the groves
the breezes
the sound of fruit dropping
the scent of citrus rot underfoot
the quiet
interrupted by crows

but not the constant
thoughts
of you

Chapter 6
Outcast

In my middle school homeroom
one girl with straight
old-fashioned bangs
and a skirt too long
is an outcast—
I know the posture
hear comments
cruel whispers
girls drop things
touched
by her
say they're
        polluted

but because of you, Ruth,
I take action
catch up
to walk with her
reaching out
as school counselors would say
letting her know I care
trying a random conversation
all those things
they told us to do

but instead of opening up to me
instead of warming to me
instead of reaching out
in return

she pivots
and walks
away

after that
not everyone is so eager
to get to know
this New Yorker
not everyone so hot
to try their English

I don't care

groups don't matter
so much to me now
maybe because I know
most atoms
aren't as stable
as they seem

every day
I watch the clock
wait for the bell
when I can be excused
mount my bike
and cycle "home"
to drink cold tea
      snack in secret
           sneak a listen
and join Koichi in the truck
blasting the radio
as we drive up
narrow tracks of steep road
high up into the groves
to work through rows of trees
thinning unneeded fruit

hours of
snapping off
and dropping fruit
snapping off
and dropping fruit
talking through branches and leaves

and
during talk
and
in between talk
thinking of you
till the five o'clock chimes

thinking
should I have said something when I saw you at the mall?
should I have sat across from you at lunch in the cafeteria?
should I have invited you to be in my group in science
or my critique partner in art?

thinking
should I have
when it seemed
by the way you
held yourself apart
that you didn't care?

when it seemed
that you didn't want me
or anyone else
to go out of our way
to have anything to do
with you?

      except
              that is
      for Jake

my legs ache
from squatting down for low branches
my arms ache
from reaching up
some days I want to chuck
the fruit
kick the rot

I don't know why my parents thought
this would be good
how they could think
it would be right
to go away
be far away
        from Emi
        from friends
        from home

but my mother
and most of Kohama
seem to agree
the solution to
any kind of problem
of any magnitude
is physical labor
sore muscles
blisters
WORK

Chapter 7
Atoms

In the evenings
before she sleeps, Yurie
lets me use her computer —
laptop on a low table,
zabuton cushion for a seat

but my evening
is early morning east coast U. S.
and no one is online at six a.m.
or seven
or even eight
except Emi

so I post on Facebook
chat with Emi
send emails to my parents
group messages to friends
my legs numb from kneeling on the cushion
as I type

and gradually we electrons
of that old atom
      connect
      regroup
      charge
      bond
a little

but it's different now
our words show restraint
we're polite
not sarcastic
considerate
not rude
we ask questions
read replies
add follow-up questions
we are caring
concerned
not ourselves
as before
as though
we're dressed up
in oversized adult clothing

Lisa, nearly not a nucleus anymore
hardly writes
homework she says
a whole summer's worth

Becca is full of Jesus
and theories of why
what happened happened

Mona jokes in half français
writes things like
the moose is king de nos forêts
the moose has une grosse tête
the male moose has un immense panache
but where before
we would have joked back
and before would have gotten mileage
from those moose
and before those moose would have turned
to secret slang between us
now we can't find
humor in a moose with a *grosse tête*
and an immense *panache*

Emily hates stocking shelves
says next year she'll lifeguard

Gina writes
and writes
poems I don't get
even when she uses
words I do get

Erin sends algebra messages
2(day) + 2(morrow) x 3(rude + x)roommates = insanity
solve for x
but only Namita sends
return equations

I tell them about the district middle school —
my uniform
kids I don't really know
outcast girl who didn't want my help
classes I don't really understand
paper fans we flap in the way too hot classroom . . .

I gripe, but only a little

all of us complain
only a little

I think we will always complain
only a little

anything more
seeming like
drama

after what happened
to you

Chapter 8
Baths

Each night here
I'm third in the bath
after Uncle and Koichi —
Baachan's orders

hot as it is in early July
I don't want a bath
just a shower
and besides
it's hard to think of climbing in the tub
after Koichi and Uncle have been in
even though they scrub clean outside the tub
just the thought of them naked in that same water . . .
well

first week I shower wash
then second week
sore from cycling to and from school
sore from afternoons of *mikan* thinning
I give in
      slip in
            soak in
water my uncle and cousin
                    soaked in
water Baachan, Aunt and Yurie will
                        soak in

heated from below
with a fire made of wood
pruned from *mikan* trees
in groves my great-grandfather began

this rectangular tub
in the bathing room off the kitchen
being the same tub
my mother soaked in
and must have
thought in
            read in
                    sulked in
                            cried in
at my age

before she knew just how far
her life would propel her
from here

afternoons
in the groves
we thin and thin
slope after slope
terrace after terrace
row after row of *mikan* trees
the dirt littered
with small green fruits

now and then
I lob one at
Koichi when
Aunt and Uncle can't see
and now and then I get
ponged on the head
or shoulder
or pelted on
my wide target
of a butt

in the truck one day Koichi says
that until I arrived
he never thought of *mikan*
as *tobidogu* — projectile weapons

I laugh
and tell him
I'm just testing
Newton's laws
the force of gravity
on horizontal velocity

some days we cut grasses
that grow fast after rains
then spread the cuttings
to control weeds —
Aunt and me with scythes
Koichi and Uncle with gas-powered
trimmers
that seem to sound even when
the motors
are off

when the noise finally fades
crows jabber
leaves rustle
cicadas whine
and hawks whistle above
us four
perched high
on mountain grove land
far above village houses
crowded at the river mouth
and fishing boats motoring
up the bay

and opposite
foothills rise
to the long volcanic slant
of Mount Fuji
that peak we see
                jutting
right through cloud
some days

and I think
if I knew you, Ruth,
and you knew me

like if this were last year
and I were here
and we were friends
and I were writing
to you

I'd tell you about that
mountaintop
        jutting

and the way the gray-blue of it
materializes from the haze
just before day becomes dusk
when the smell
of smoke
from wood fires
for all the baths
fills the air

Chapter 9
Hats

Whenever they spray
pesticide or herbicide
or whatever it is
I'm told to stay below
to help Baachan
garden in vegetable plots
that lie across the stream
that divides the village

we stop at houses to offer greetings
to second cousins
third cousins
great-uncles
great-aunts
who compare me to my mother
speak highly of my mother
but rarely mention
my father

they serve us chilled barley tea
and a sweet
to sustain us before we
duck out into the sun
to weed

Baachan outfits me—
smock
wrist covers
gloves
baggy pants
and a huge
flower-print
bonnet
with visor
and neck ruffle

I complain
but she won't stand
for my Yankees cap, a gift
from my dad one summer
not enough coverage
Baachan says and
double-knots
the bonnet ties
under my chin

very first time in that getup
I take a picture
email it to my mother

and the next week
in a packet
in the mailbox
is an all-sport sun hat
that Koichi and Uncle
covet

I ask my mother to send two more

which she does
express

but Baachan says the hats were wasteful
scowls through dinner
the day they are delivered
interrupts
to change the subject
if anyone
dares
ask me a question or
draw me into
conversation

upstairs
Yurie tells me not to worry
I expect her to go on
say
Baachan's a stubborn old fool
or something in my defense

but she sides with her
says
Baachan's lived through hard times
in a farm household
where nothing is thrown out
everything recycled
and no item purchased
       unless absolutely necessary

I roll my eyes
but Yurie frowns
says
it's due to Baachan's ways
that the farm's a success
that she could study pharmacology
that Koichi could specialize
in agricultural mechanical technology
that Uncle could purchase additional lands
that they could open their home
this summer
to me

in the bath
I fume
and sulk
and curse you, Ruth,
for sticking me here
with cheapskate relatives
and ancestors always hovering
in the altar
and I wonder

how will I make it through
nearly two more months
in this village
so far from everything?

Chapter 10
Faults

Y ou'd think the way they talk
and don't talk about certain things
around here that it was
my father's fault
my mother left the farm

but she'd decided sometime
in her last year of high school
she would study abroad

so when she failed
her college entrance exams
instead of studying to take them again
she took a job
at the district agricultural office
that she could cycle to
from the farm
and for two years
saved
her money

then, despite Baachan's
and Jiichan's protests
despite warnings
from aunts, uncles
and villagers
but with encouragement
from an escapee cousin
in Queens

she flew to New York
moved in with three
other Japanese
taking advantage of
the late-eighties
bubble-era
crazy days
of plenty
of yen

she took classes at a
community college and
worked at a Japanese restaurant
where she rose to rank of hostess
and learned to wear kimono
and walk and bow and hold herself
like farm girls generally don't

and where she seated my father
at the same street-facing window table
for lunch every
Sushi Fair! Wednesday
his routine escape
from the rigors
of law school

it wasn't his fault that
as he gathered his notes
from the tabletop one afternoon
she confided in him
that someday she, too
hoped to attend
university

to study what? he'd asked

plant science she'd hastily replied
then laughed
suddenly
wildly
hysterically

what's so funny? he'd asked
I grew up on a farm! she said
so? he said
I'm here in New York she said
so? he said
no green! no plants! she said

and because he didn't get the joke
that by then had her clutching her
obi-bound sides
he'd asked her
if she would join him
for brunch
in Brooklyn
on Sunday

which is when she first had
an everything bagel
with cream cheese
and lox

here in Kohama
no one says so but I know
they blame my father
for taking my mother

but my mother says it
was the fault of the lox
that after she ate the lox
bit through the softness of
salmon with slivers of onion
she looked at this man
my father
and listened
to everything he had to say
about anything
understanding only
one quarter of what he had to say
about anything

but those were the days
before U.S. orange imports into Japan
when village *mikan* brought in good money
and Jiichan was able to lure my mother home
with promises rare for a fourth daughter
that he had yen left over
to help her start a business
that he would purchase land
for hothouses
for her

so my mother
understanding at last
her love for plants
and growing things,
and thinking she owed her father gratitude,
and thinking my father
  a law student who loved
  not plants but
  ideas and debate
didn't fit her future,
returned to Kohama
worked at the agricultural office again
harvested *mikan*
and planned a business raising
salad greens and heirloom vegetables

even now when we're walking
through the village
Baachan sometimes says

your mother planned to put her
first hothouses here
or
your mother had her eyes
on that plot there
or
that man standing over there
had planned to ask your mother
to marry him

but within a year
after passing the bar exam
my father caught a plane to Narita
found his way to the city of Numazu
took a bus to this *mikan* district
arrived
in Kohama
unannounced
unknown
asking at the gasoline stand
owned by my grandfather's brother
for the home of
Sachiko Mano

Emi and I always loved the tale
the daring
the nerve
but Jiichan and Baachan
never forgave the surprise
of this man
who our mother
had never mentioned
to anyone in Kohama
until he appeared
in the driveway
and dropped to one knee
speaking words of English
even Baachan understood
even Jiichan guessed
and words of Japanese
he'd practiced for weeks
in night classes

they married three weeks later
held a party paid for
from my father's savings
in Kohama's village hall
followed several months after that
by a quiet ceremony
and brunch reception
in Brooklyn
with bagels and lox

they moved to the far suburbs
of New York City
upstate
they joked
to buy a small house with
enough land for plots
of Asian vegetables

I arrived
after hothouses had been built
soil was compost rich
Sachi's Farm had been born
and my mother was marketing her first
Japanese pumpkins and edible luffa

Emi followed
in the year the daikon grew
long as two-year-old me

visits from New York
back to Kohama
started when I was three
but by age seven
I could tell
things were strained —
us staying
not at this house
not with Jiichan and Baachan
Aunt, Uncle and first cousins Koichi and Yurie
but in homes of second cousins
and once, even
an inn

not till the start of Jiichan's cancer
when my mother tutored us
for months before
bringing us over
to help
to behave
and make amends

not until then
did we sleep at this house
did we get treated like family
did Jiichan have a good thing to say
about my father
or Emi
or me

that was when Jiichan
on his good days
taught me how to dig clams
for soup
how to sharpen a knife
on a stone
and clean and scale
aji fish by the pump
in the driveway

and how to make a viewer
for seeing underwater
      damselfish
      anemones
      sea slugs
      crabs
along the shore beyond the pier
when I didn't have a mask and snorkel

and that was when I began
to understand
there are at least
two sides to any story
that Jiichan had been mean
because he hurt
that he blamed
because he grieved
for a daughter
leaving

fault and blame —
both seem so easy to place
but much harder
maybe
to erase

I think
there must be at least
two sides
to your story, too, Ruth,

and maybe knowing
more of Lisa's side
how she lived with
her godparents
not her parents
who were I don't know where
might help explain
why she was so mean
to you

and why we all
followed
her lead

Chapter 11
Gifts

Dusk one evening
my Kohama second cousin
Asuka
high school student
calls on us

proper, like
phone call first
formal front-door visit
with summer gift presented to Uncle
who hands it to Baachan
who places it before the Buddhist altar
for Jiichan and the ancestors

by now I know the routine
and rise to do my part to
serve cold barley tea
chilled fruit
and small cakes
after which I
sit at the edge
of conversation

Asuka turns to me and says
do you remember me?
but I don't
until she says
you stayed with us
when you were little!

and then I remember
the girl cousin who went off to school
while Emi and I stayed
at the house or followed
our mother on visits or errands
around the village

Asuka would return
in the afternoons
with homework
she'd do kneeling at a low table
and I would sit beside her
waiting
watching her make pencil strokes
in columns of *kanji* boxes
and sometimes
she would let me write
in her drill book

I stare at her
and finally
when she laughs
at my puzzlement
I see a resemblance to
the Asuka back then

but now Asuka
gets to the point
of her visit tonight
and invites me
to join her
and some friends
on the Marine Day
long weekend—

day trip to Tokyo

Baachan scowls
frets the cost
clucks and starts to lecture

I'm ready to protest
but under the table
Aunt holds my wrist
then speaks up
to assure Baachan
that I have my own funds for travel
that I will be chaperoned by Asuka
and, besides, I will benefit
from a day trip to the capital
visited only once
with my family
when Emi was small enough
to be carried
on my father's shoulders

a photo album
that Aunt pulls
from a shelf
provides proof
and finally
as we laugh at snapshots of all of us
much much younger

Baachan says
she supposes
I can go

Asuka claps
and winks
at me

I like Asuka
her smooth and
natural manners
the way she addresses
Baachan with deference
but includes me with
smiling eyes

she's two years older
but makes me feel
at ease
makes me feel
I can just be me
for a change

and that maybe with her
I will stop thinking
of you

the Marine Day long weekend
marks the end of the school term
end of my four weeks
at the middle school
and I'm not sorry to say good-bye
      to friends I never made
      classes I couldn't always follow
      conversations about TV shows I don't know
      borrowed textbooks
      sailor uniform
           white kneesocks
                 uwabaki indoor shoes

not sorry, that is, until
students in my homeroom throw
a surprise farewell party
sing songs for me
present me with a class photo
and a basket full of origami
            birds, cicadas
                    frogs, flowers, hearts
                            and Pokémon characters
plus a placard signed
with all their names

they tell me not to forget them
set out mini donuts they decorated
chips, cookies and drinks they bought
with their own spending money

one girl cries
and even outcast girl
hangs around
and in the end
hands me a present —
a cell phone strap with a tiny
mikan
charm

Chapter 12
Rapport

From then on I work full days on the farm—

up at six
in the groves by eight
break before noon
down to the house for lunch
up to the groves by one
      or two if the heat's too high
done by five

we use shears to snip
the fruit, now large
as Ping-Pong balls

my arms no longer ache
my back and shoulders
feel strong
but the day is long

and when conversation stops
among the leaves
and it's just the breathing
of wind in trees
and the *mee-mee-mee-meeen*
of cicadas
there is much
too much
time
for my thoughts

and moments when I have to pause
catch my breath
hold on to a branch
and not because I'm tired
or lost my balance
but because I'm seeing you, Ruth,

alone

in Osgoods' orchard

setting down your pack
having chosen
your tree

everyone knows
Lisa didn't mean it
everyone knows
when a person says
certain things
they don't mean
the words
they say
really

in the note you left
for your parents
and brother
you said
life was too hard
they could never know
what it was like
for you
at school
where you were ostracized
                    left out
                    despised

and where
just that day
in front of all us girls
after Jake handed you
a piece of paper

Lisa had given you
a look
and said

I hope you die

I saw you glare
at Lisa

hard, I thought
mean, I thought
bitch we all said

hurt, I now realize
as you crumpled that note into a
tiny ball
that was still
in your jeans pocket
when you were found
in Osgoods' orchard

here in Kohama
under the *mikan* trees
sometimes I see you
over there
among the apple trees

and I think how
after the graveside service
as we left the cemetery
Jake's mom told my mom
and Gina's mom
that you once told Jake
you loved orchards
the rhythm of the year
in sap, leaves, buds, fruit
the cycle of growth and rest
growth and rest

and how Gina and I then shared looks
and wondered
just how often you'd been there
with him
and wondered
what else we hadn't known
about Jake
        and you
                and trees

she said you'd visit on your way home
from piano lessons
that you
and Jake
had a
rapport

now in my too much time
in the groves
I think maybe
I ought to write to Jake
email him

not to press him for more
background
or information
or understanding
or to draw him out

but to tell him
thank you
for giving you
that
at least —
rapport

Chapter 13
Tokyo

Sunday morning early
Asuka picks me up
and her father drives us
and her friends Rika and Ai
to the nearest train station
from where we ride a few stops
switch to an express and we are

zooming
off the peninsula
away from the
farms
        orchards
                villages
                        ancestors

we play cards on the way
plan our day
share salty snacks
sweet snacks
take pictures
trade listens on music players
of favorite singers and bands
talk and talk and
then we are there

Tokyo

Ai leads the way as we change trains
then switch to subway
and get off by a temple
with a giant lantern
and stalls of crafts and paper goods
and *ningyoyaki* cakes shaped
like pigeons and pagodas

then Rika, anime freak
drags us to the place for manga
and crowds of geeky gamers
and electronics
and blasting advertisements
and cosplayers
but Asuka rescues us

gets us on another
subway that takes us across town
to a ritzy treelined street of
designer shops
at the end of which is
Harajuku with tiny shops
for jewelry, hair stuff, bags and clothes
that we try on and on
though none
none
fit right
on me

we eat cheap
convenience store
rice triangles, noodles,
take a too-long walk
through woods
to a somber shrine
where we toss money in the box
and pray or
act like we're praying
then look at
amulets for sale

I buy one for Emi
that's good for success at school
then Ai speaks up
and reaches over our heads to buy
five tiny golden pouches
that guard good fortune
happiness
luck

one for each
of us
and Emi, too

leaving the shrine
and the woods
we get on a train
and just one stop later
get off the train
then head into people
and a crossing
with crowds so thick I

    panic

hold Asuka's hand
and Rika holds mine
and Ai hers
as we try to reach
Shibuya 109

where because of speakers
blasting different songs
and shouting
and crazy shoving
and reaching through racks of clothes
we start to fade
leave the shops
find a curry restaurant
then a café
for cake

we end with Tokyo Tower
where Asuka
treats us to an extra ticket
for the elevator up
        to the highest level
for sunset —
soft, rose-gray
subdued
by haze

dusk drops
over the city
below us
soon with lights
everywhere
ablaze

on the train back
we talk
compare photos
take more
talk more
exchange email addresses
doze

Uncle meets us at the station in Koichi's car
delivers Asuka and her friends
to homes in different villages
spread out along the quiet coast

so dark
and silent
after pulsing Tokyo

I thank him
there in the truck
as we wind our way
along the shore
the only lights
the bright lights
of squid boats
offshore

bowing deeply
my head thumps
the dashboard
as I tell him it was
a great day
yokatta I say
honto ni yokatta
really, truly great

and Uncle smiles for me
on the night of the first day
since before it all happened
that I did not
think of you

Chapter 14
Projects

Koichi went to agriculture school
but specialized in
mechanical technology
loves to work on the tractor
for uprooting old trees
fix the grass trimmers
putter with his car
invent new tools, do carpentry . . .
for him *mikan* are just an excuse for
machines, equipment, vehicles

he gets it when I mention physics
uses the Japanese terms
I'm picking up from manga
to talk about laws of motion
forces and acceleration
body A
interacting with
body B

he quizzes me
makes me explain
till he's sure
I get it in English and
in Japanese

one day when it rains off and on
and Uncle says *can't go up there*
meaning the groves
I help Koichi repair a storage shed
in a flat lower grove
that was a paddy
when Baachan was young
when the village had
fewer *mikan* trees
and grew its own rice

we remove rotted planking
nail in "new" lumber
recycled from a tear-down
and patch the roof
then he gives me
a problem to solve —

how to brace
the leaning rear wall

he says to design a plan
so with a stick
in the dirt
I draw a rock foundation
supporting an extension
of floor beams
joined by a board
to make an L
into a triangle

if it fails it's your fault
he says, grinning

but he follows my plan
exactly

with Koichi
working on the shed
solving a building problem
I'm here in Kohama
just here
in the zone
of a project

but when the weather clears
and we return to the trees
      thinning
      snipping
      pruning
my hand a machine
on automatic
my mind wanders
and I see you again
and I'm back in those days
right after

the day after the morning
you were found
school was open as usual
but with special homeroom meetings
where anyone who hadn't heard
through the grapevine
or the school website
learned the news
and where counselors told us
no one was to blame

but in less than a week
as the investigation began
and talk traveled
and letters to editors were printed
and gossip spread
in supermarkets and banks
we could tell
that people around town
and beyond our town
blamed
us eighth-grade girls

our sadness for you
turned then, Ruth,
our hurting changed to anger
for doing what you did

they were just words, Ruth,
what Lisa said
you didn't have to listen
to words

four words
hurled in
jealousy

to get you out of my head
I ask Koichi for other challenges
and after the success of the shed
he finds more problems for me to solve —

how to distribute sacks of fertilizer
over a mountain grove of
      eight terraces
      twelve trees long
      two trees deep in places
      one in others

how best to bundle, transport and store pruned wood
how to repair a bridge across a washout
improve air circulation in storehouses
repair sorting bins
enlarge the rooftop laundry deck . . .

when I'm busy
when I think and plan and talk
calculate and estimate
and use my hands
to work the different tools

then I can keep
thoughts of you
at bay
and I'm okay
being here
at the end of July
on this farm
in my old clothes

Chapter 15
Sisters

On the phone one night
when my mother calls
Aunt tells her I've been no trouble
Yurie says I'm a good roommate
Koichi praises my work
and after he hands the phone to me
and I explain projects he's mentioned
my mother sounds surprised
by my enthusiasm
since I never was enthused
at home helping
at Sachi's Farm

I didn't know you were a farmer she jokes
I hope you did your schoolwork properly she says
I hope you aren't being a bother she frets

I tell her I'm done with school
I like the grove work just fine
then I try to turn the questions
on her
and her summer helpers
and blueberry and raspberry yields

Emi rescues me
takes the phone
and chatters
till she's out of
Mom's hearing
then whispers
daijobu? —you okay?
don't you do it, too!

I think she's talking farming
me becoming a farmer
and I'm about to say
I just might

then I realize what she means
by "it"
iyada! I say —
no way!

but for the rest of our conversation
worry seeps into her voice
and missing into mine
as we ask about
what we've each
been doing
this summer
apart

when my father takes the phone
he bellows
like I'm deaf
get good and strong!
JV soccer tryouts
day after you return!
I hold the phone far from my ear
and roll my eyes

Yurie smiles
and we laugh
like sisters
sort of

but later
in my head
I hear Emi's worry
far into the night
when I lie
alone
next to Yurie, sleeping

and lying there alone
thinking of you
I remember

it wasn't until a group session
with counselors
the week after
that Jake
spoke up and explained
that his sister was bipolar
that you'd told him
you thought you
were bipolar
that you were new
to the darkness
of depression
the lows after the highs
the highs after the lows
that you hadn't told anyone
and that he told you there were meds
that could help

and that the note
that you crumpled into your pocket
after Lisa's four words
had the name of his
sister's doctor

and I remember how
the counselor
said something about
not commenting
on cause or diagnosis
but that ninety percent
of people who do
what you did
suffer from an illness like depression

it wasn't until then
right then
that everyone began seeing
your side of the story—
you

Chapter 16
Evidence

Baachan makes me cook now
makes me take
Yurie's place
preparing breakfast
in the mornings

I learn to prepare miso soup
Baachan-style with wakame
and horse mackerel
Uncle-style with ginger
how to peel, slice, chop and grate
cucumbers, carrots, daikon
and burdock
just so

140

her shadow looming as
she hovers
to correct my grip on the knife
or adjust the thickness of a slice
or fix the angle of a cut
or arrangement
on a plate

she teaches me
pickling
drying
preserving
of vegetables and fruits
even fish
split, gutted and salt dried in
mesh nets that we hang from
laundry poles

not that I will use
this knowledge in New York where
our garden has so much more than
standard Japanese varieties and
my mother insists on fresh, not pickled —
too much salt for your father, she says

Baachan also corrects my mannerisms
assesses my gestures
notes my posture
and ways of sitting
or standing
and likes to tweak
my never
polite enough
Japanese

and every day
she reminds me
of the eighty-percent rule
of eating

determined
to send me home
thin

she seems to think I need to eat
less American and
more Japanese
that I eat too much meat
fries, pancakes and
bad American food

I tell her we never eat fries
I tell her we often eat vegetarian
I tell her we eat
Russian
Jewish
Italian
Mexican
Japanese
Chinese
Korean
Middle Eastern
Greek
even Ethiopian . . .
I tell her I don't know what she means
by bad American food

but she says
look
and points to
my butt
as evidence

Chapter 17
Blink

Uncle sends me to help Koichi
spread fertilizer in the steepest grove
one where there's a monorail track to carry
equipment up
and *mikan* off
the mountain

Koichi and I load bags of fertilizer
onto the flatbed cart
he fiddles with the motor
pull starts till it throbs to life
and shouts at me to climb on
he'll walk

the cart labors slowly up the incline
of track and I'm leaning far back
my face pointed up to the sky
loving it

passing Koichi
walking up the grove path
I wave, holler
eat my dust!
a phrase I taught him
in the truck
and he laughs

I watch terraces of trees go by
then off to the side
a metal pole
and from the pole a string
and hanging from the string
a black thing
fabric, I think
scarecrow, I think

crow
I see
when it blinks

then I'm off the cart and Koichi's running
to cut the motor
and catch up to where I'm yelling
beneath the pole
while above me
hanging
tied by one leg
the blinking crow
sways
in the breeze

Koichi tries to explain
it's to scare the other crows away
the fish smell of the fertilizer
they're attracted to it!

but I scream
ikiteiru —
it's alive!

and I climb the pole
hand over hand
like I learned climbing ropes
in gym
with you
hand over hand
till I reach the top
and with pruning shears from
my tool belt
cut
through the string

the crow falls

thuds
on the ground

I slide down the pole
and the half-dead crow
turns its head
blinks
as I approach
but Koichi from behind me
brings a shovel down
on that head
so it rings

I'm on Koichi then, belting him
trying to grab the shovel
to kill *him*
till we're on the ground, rolling
away from the now-dead crow
I claw at Koichi's face but he pins me
in the dirt
holds me down hard
till the fight leaves me
and I curl up
trembling
and sounds come
sirenlike
from my mouth

finally
I stand

I walk down the slope
stalk back to the village
into the house

I won't speak to him
won't speak to any of them
just lie on my futon
facing the wall
iPod on

later
I rise to the
five o'clock chimes
and go against the tide of
farmers coming down the hills
and climb up past the temple and the
cemetery where Jiichan's ashes are
to the slope of bamboo that used to be
harvested for laundry poles, scaffolding and tools
but now is almost never cut and grows thick
invading forests
on either side

I climb up
beneath knocking trunks
slipping on dry bamboo leaves
scrambling up to the top of the grove
where it turns suddenly to cedar again
dark and quiet and soft underfoot
until that ends and I hit the mixed forest
of the ridge and a path that Jiichan
once showed me
and Koichi said is still there
and leads to a rock in a clearing
with a view
of the bay

I follow the ridge
which is the edge of the village
just like I remember doing with Jiichan
that time we visited when he'd just turned ill
but still had strength
and sure enough I find the rock
and climb up onto its back
needing that view
that bay
that mountain
but Koichi must not have been there in a while
or at least not in summer
'cause all I see
are trees

so I slip and slide back down
through cedar and bamboo
landing hard on my oversized butt
that Baachan doesn't understand
won't shrink even if she starves me
and I find the family grave
and sit down on a low wall
and face the bay
the far shore, the blue
peak of Mount Fuji
with its upper
west slopes
still lit by sun
and I just
breathe

I don't talk to Jiichan
don't believe in that stuff
but I wish he were here
to sit with me

silent

as the night shadow
climbs Mount Fuji

after dark I go back
walk right past them in the kitchen
return to my futon

and even when Baachan comes in
tugs the earbuds out of my ears
tells me to get into the bath
I don't speak to her
just get my pajamas
towel
and go

even when I'm back upstairs
and Yurie brings dinner
on a tray
and I don't eat a thing
except rice
and some boiled peanuts
even then
I don't say
a word

when I finally stomp downstairs
I tell them I will write
to the *New York Times*
the *Japan Times*
every *Times* in the world
about the way they
treat crows
if they don't quit
that custom
and make everyone else
in the village
quit that custom now

the farm is connected
to a cooperative
that's part of
an agricultural organization
they can do this
I think

still
I'm surprised when
Uncle bows
Koichi bows
and they say
they are sorry
for upsetting me
and they will use
other ways to scare the crows
from now on

that night I read till late
Physics and You
general relativity
maximum force
kinetic energy
conservation
of energy
mass dependence
reversing the motion

and biographies of
Marie Curie
Alfred Nobel
and Hideyo Noguchi

then in the dark
I lie
iPod on
trying not to picture
you
trying not to recall
the crow
trying not to see
that blink

Chapter 18
Stupid

After that
I write to Jake
figuring
what's to lose

not email
but a real letter
on folded paper
in an envelope
and a close-enough address

even though no one
that I know of
from the atom
has dared
to write him
or email him
or text him
in New York
where he's counselor-in-training
at the nature camp
outside town

I think you should know, Ruth,
those last weeks of school
after you did
what you did
on his family's land
while he slept
inside his room
not fifty yards
away

he kept to himself
away from even
Noah and Ken
who used to always
be at his side

all those weeks
he studied alone
ran track
broke school records
and never spoke
to us

stupid spiteful girls

his words
as he left one of the
counseling sessions
those first days after

that was when I got mad
stood, shouted
we're not stupid!
ran out of that classroom after him
yelled at him
yelled at teachers and counselors
coming after me
and asked
where the hell were you?

what I wanted to know was
if depression is so common
if depression was a possibility
for someone like you, Ruth,
then why didn't they teach us about it?

where were the experts to tell
stupid spiteful us
about social withdrawal
and mania
and gestures
and impulsiveness
and all the signs
that we might have
been able to interpret
to understand you?

in my letter to Jake
I want to ask why
he didn't clue us in

did he think we'd just know?
did he think we'd just get it?

or did you ask him
not to say anything
to us
or to Lisa
about why you were
sometimes seen
with him?

but then I think of that word
rapport
and how I'd had to look it up
that night after the service
when Jake's mom said it
and how maybe Jake was right
that we were
stupid spiteful girls

I do my best
not to sound
stupid
in my letter

use words that
show signs of
a fledgling
brain

I ride the bicycle
to take the letter to the post office
but when I go to buy a stamp
I see display sheets of 80-yen stamps
     world heritage
     anime heroes
     calligraphy
     wild boars
and even though it takes 110 yen
for a letter to the States
and even though I'm partial to
one anime heroine
I buy a sheet of 80-yen stamps
of the fiftieth anniversary
of the Japanese Antarctic research expedition

emperor penguins and seals
the *Soya* research ship
and Taro, brother of Jiro
two Sakhalin husky
survivors

hoping that two Antarctic research stamps
about the real expedition
and not the expedition made up
by Disney
will show
I'm not
stupid

Chapter 19
Dance

One evening after farmwork
we rush through dinner and
Aunt cleans up while
Yurie tugs at my arms
and pulls me
to the village hall parking lot
to practice Bon dances

one dance I'd learned
at Japanese weekend school
another I know vaguely
from my mother
who'd play a cassette
and make Emi and me
and my father
follow her
around the living room
some summers
she was homesick

but other songs and dances
are new to me
performed in a circle
to music on a CD
that they restart
and track back
again and again
to help newbies like me learn
where to put their feet
when to go forward
when backward
when to raise the fan and
when
to stop

Asuka dances, too
and after practice
she and Yurie and I sit
with cold canned tea
handed out by the
village women's association
and as people drift off
for home
we talk

Yurie leaves when
she's done with her tea
but Asuka and I
stay longer
till she and I are
the only ones left
and Asuka asks
about my friends
and New York
and how far is the city
from our town
and Manhattan and Broadway
and shopping and
I promise to show her around
if she comes to visit

each night
we gather
we dance
wave our fans
wave our arms
stepping forward
stepping back
then Asuka and I talk
sitting on the gritty boards
of that strip of veranda
by the darkened village hall
after everyone goes home

and I think
I'm glad to have
this cousin friend

and I think
to tell Asuka
about you
someday

Chapter 20
Preparations

Obon comes to Kohama
and work stops
for us
but not for Yurie—
pharmacies in the city of Numazu
never closing
for the odd Obon dates
on this quiet part of the peninsula

like all farm families here
for Jiichan
great-grandfather
and other ancestor spirits
we set up the special altar
to welcome them home

Uncle assembles a wood frame
floor to ceiling with
planks set in for a table
like a food stall
at a fair

Aunt covers the planks with
grass blades cut to forearm length
then from a rod we drape
persimmon sprigs
abundant, unthinned clusters
of green *mikan* — eight, nine
even ten to a bunch —
taro stalks and leaves
edamame
more taro stalks and leaves
more persimmon sprigs
more *mikan*
harvest greens

Uncle sets out the memorial tablet
Baachan brings water for the spirits
then in armloads
from the kitchen table
where they are heaped
we carry a watermelon, a pumpkin, grapes
peaches, corn, chestnuts
dry *somen* noodles
even Jiichan's favorite black sugar candies
and we set them all
atop the blades of grass

we hang the family scroll
names of deceased
going back generations
and in front of everything
place an eggplant cow
and cucumber horse
for the spirits
to ride home

I think of Sukkoth
and you
sitting under an abundance
of fall harvest
in a backyard sukkah
as you must have done
as I do
with my father and mother
and Emi each fall
my mother loving that
Jewish festival
that reminds her so much
of Kohama
Obon

Koichi and I then assemble
an outside altar
on a post
like a birdhouse
that we cover with greens

and into which Baachan sets
another cup of water
and bowl of rice
for Jiichan

we hang a lantern
under the roof eave
to guide him home
and Baachan sighs

next morning
Baachan makes me light incense
ring the bell
and think a prayer
before the priest comes
to chant sutras

then after the priest departs
to do his rounds
in the village
and the district
up and down
the entire coast
I'm told
I have the day off to do
whatever
I want

so I take the three-speed bike out
of the garage
and Koichi sees me
asks where I'm going
and I say *that way* —
I've never been to the cape
and he says
I'll go with you
finds a bike with deflated tires
that he inflates and tests
and grabs two thermoses
of cold tea
and then we are off
me leading
Koichi following
out of Kohama

we ride through *mikan*
and fishing villages
one after another
to the farthest west cape
of hotels and dive shops
where we leave our bikes
walk to a small shrine
then follow a path
out the arm of the cape
that takes us to . . .
a pond?

> freshwater
> with koi
> crazy close
> to the sea

and gnarled twisted trees
that Koichi says are
treasures over a thousand years old
though I don't know how
they could have stood for so long
on a narrow strip of land
constantly battered by waves
wind
and typhoons

at the tip of rocky cape
we sit to drink from our thermoses
and gaze across the bay to a stubborn
Mount Fuji
that refuses to budge
from the haze

then from rock to rock
we hop and leap around
waves slapping and crashing
at our feet as we poke through
washed-up trash

Koichi finds a rubber ball
we play catch with
and I find a small bucket
and in it put
smooth round rocks

after we loop back
we stop at a beach hut
and Koichi orders
lemon soda
for me
beer for him

and we listen to divers talk about oxygen tanks
and lessons
and fish
and Koichi asks lots of questions
and I can tell he wants to learn to dive
and I'm thinking I'd like to try that, too

going down into the sea
to find gliding
darting
colors
just
for fun

Chapter 21
Spirits

Late afternoon when the sun
has dropped behind the hills
west of Kohama
we light a small welcome fire
by the entrance of the house
to guide the spirits

I think
with all the signs
we have left
there is no way
Jiichan will go astray and
not be able
to find us

we walk past other welcome fires
set along the river, on the bridge, in driveways
and head uphill to the temple and cemetery
where we fill a bucket with water
climb the hillside of graves
full of villagers
and visitors
all with buckets of
sloshing
water

Uncle lights incense
and hands us each some sticks
and I do whatever
Aunt and Koichi and Yurie do
place some incense
in a part of the stone
and pray with other sticks
to my ancestors
even though officially
these ancestors
are no longer mine
my mother being outside of
and no longer part of
this Mano family line

still, outsider or not
I help drizzle water on greens
and into vases

and on the polished stone
I place tiny piles of
rice and minced eggplant
nourishment
for spirits

we walk downhill
to the pier
where reflected in
the water are
more welcome fires
torches lit
for all the spirits
to be sure
they find their way

these spirits who must be
hopeless
with directions

Chapter 22
Visitors

Next day an aunt arrives
second-eldest sister of my mother
with her husband
and their son Kota,
their other son Yuta
having gone off
with university friends to
an island somewhere
to snorkel and kayak

Kota seems to wish he, too
were on an island
somewhere
anywhere

Baachan issues orders
about serving tea and
squares of fruit *kanten*
and a bowl of purple grapes
that I set out on the table
in the receiving room
by the special Obon altar
all decorated
with vegetables
and greens

later I ask Kota why they aren't visiting his father's family
and Kota says that his father is third son
and his mother second daughter
they are a new branch family
and no one has died
so they are
free

I'm told to take Kota
to wander the festival stalls
near the village hall but
there is nothing really for us
just booths
for catching goldfish
and yoyos
and a few arcade games
for little kids

so we buy a couple of
dripping cold sodas
and walk out to the pier
past small piles of burned sticks
and ash from the welcome fires
and I tell him I think it would
just be easier to give
the spirits GPS-activated
cell phones

Kota laughs
and we sit down on
an overturned boat
and drink our sodas
but it's too hot out there
on the pier so we
walk along other docks
following the high-tide line
to where the shore gets wider
and sit down in an arc of shade
made from a rise of sandstone cliff
that climbs behind us
and leans out
over us
precariously
toward the water

Kota pulls a music player
from a pocket
gives me one earbud
and him the other
and we sit there on the rocks by the sea
        which seems to have been stilled
        by this first-day-of-August heat
listening to songs
looking over the water

it's like there is no opposite
northern shore today
like the bay
is really the Pacific
the haze is so thick

I tell him that Mount Fuji
really is there
right there
and he says
sure
sarcastic

then he says
but summer's no good for Fuji-san anyway
you have to see it with its snowcap
in winter

which may be true
but I still like it
even blue-gray
faint
and barely there
in summer

I ask what year he is
and he says *middle school third*
so he's one ahead of me
but since he attends a combined
middle and high school
he doesn't have to take
high school entrance exams
and study all this summer

I ask if he likes it there in Shimizu
and he shrugs
every day school, basketball
school, basketball
he says
I could be anywhere

then Kota asks about
my time in Kohama
so far

I start to tell him
little bits about
the district middle school
the *mikan* work
the projects with Koichi

but then I realize
he's only half listening

I stop
wait
and he says

aren't you here 'cause someone died?

I sit there stunned
so used to
no one
around me
talking about you

and then I have to stand
and turn
and face the cliff
and its eroded contours
because I am crying

Kota waits
and when I finally turn back
and walk over to where the sea
just barely laps the rocks
and lean down for a handful of water
to wash off my face
and sit down again
not far from him
he says he's sorry

I shake my head
to mean
it's okay

then he asks
was it a friend?

and I think
then weigh my words
and answer softly
adding the helping verb *hazu*

tomodachi no hazu datta

she should have been
was supposed to have been
a friend

.

for a while
we just sit there
staring at the still water

then we head back
to the festival stalls
and Kota pays money
says *watch this*
and with a circle of paper net
dips and slides and turns and catches
three goldfish
that he carefully drops into
a plastic bag
of water

and after he ties the string
shut
he holds them up
between us
and hands the
bag of flashing
darting orange
to me

Chapter 23
One Hundred Eight

That evening we all go down
to the seawall
and watch
as Koichi with the other men
of the fire brigade
in *happi* coats and headbands
ignite the wood
for 108 fires

the number being symbolic
in Buddhism
for 108 things like
greed
pride
ignorance
egoism
jealousy
cruelty
deceit
rage
that must be overcome
to reach Nirvana

but since it's the second night
of Obon I ask
are these
welcoming or
sending-off fires

after a moment
Baachan says
both

so I ask
but won't that confuse the spirits?

and she says
they can come and go
as they please
with their free schedules

and I realize that Baachan
has actually attempted
a joke

108 fires
burn
blaze
spark
and snap

the flames leaping
and heating our feet
legs and hands

warming the faces
of villagers
perched and
illuminated
there on the seawall
above the pier

when the fires die
the fire brigade guys
sweep the ash
into the bay
and everyone jumps down
from the wall
and heads to the village hall lot
to sing
and dance
some of the dances
we've practiced
and compete
in a rock-paper-scissors contest
where I win . . .

a melon

and walking back to the house
cradling my melon
I wonder

if we could issue invitations
send word to spirits
from other lands and languages
to come midsummer
to this shore opposite Mount Fuji
and find the village
with the three needle-like rocks
that poke up by the river mouth
and locate the row of 108 fires along
a pier that juts out from this village
into Suruga Bay

if we could invite
distant spirits
to join in
the celebrations
here

and if I did
invite you, Ruth

well?
would you come?

Chapter 24
Good

The next morning
Uncle doesn't let us sleep in
but hollers us
awake at six
when Yurie is getting ready
to go to work
which is way too early
for a holiday

we cram into two cars
and drive up into the hills
to do a ridge walk
along a path to the
nearest peak

from the parking lot
to the summit
is only an hour's walk
but we hardly talk the whole way
everyone in a straggly line
groggy
      and sweaty
            and cranky
                  and hungry
but when we reach the summit
we can see the sea
east and west,
and to the north
Mount Fuji, one side
still morning rouge
and to the south
rolling on
nearly forever
the swishing *sasa* grass
and mountains
of this peninsula

Uncle sets out a plastic sheet
and Baachan and both aunts
set out a picnic breakfast
of rice balls
and pickles
and fried chicken
and fruit
and salad
and there is coffee
and tea
and canned *mikan* juice
and everyone
gradually
comes to life

and there
at nearly a thousand meters
above the sea and higher
than just about everything

I feel
I could practically wave
at you

later, back at the house
I help with laundry
and kitchen cleanup
and prepare more foods
to set out later
whenever people are hungry

feeling sorry for Yurie
having to work
and wanting to do what I can
to be sure she
doesn't have to work more
when she gets home

then when it is still afternoon
when Uncle and
other uncle and
Kota have gone off
Baachan makes me bathe
and upstairs makes me
dress in kimono underclothes
and kneel on a cushion
while she does my hair
up
and back
and pinned too tight with ornaments

then Yurie
gets home from the pharmacy
sees my hair and
takes it down
and does it
up
and back
and pinned again with ornaments
        but better
                with hair spray
                and gel

Baachan, Yurie and my aunts
then present me with
a *yukata* kimono
of morning glories
that Aunt has sewn
from fabric they bought
and an obi long as the room
that Baachan tugs, folds, bends
into a bow
tied tight around my waist
Baachan announcing to all
that she must add
extra towel stuffing
to straighten my figure and
compensate
for my extra-wide
oversized
butt

Yurie dresses in *yukata,* too
a single thin towel
enough
to straighten her
slim figure

downstairs
we find
Kota is waiting
now smiling
he, too, in a *yukata*
men's style

photos are snapped
indoors
outdoors
in all combinations of
cousins and aunts and uncles and Baachan
even one with me in the center
of everyone
holding my bowl of
darting orange
goldfish

then Kota, Yurie and I
step our feet into *geta*
and shuffle out to the village hall parking lot
now strung with paper lanterns
now with music blaring
now full of the village and visitors
and Koichi and the fire brigade
then Aunt, Uncle
other aunt and uncle
and Baachan
and cousins I've met
cousins I've maybe met
neighbors I've seen
neighbors I've never seen
we all dance circles of
Bon dances

later I send pictures to
Mom, Dad and Emi

and Emi emails
you look so
Japanese!

and my mother emails
yokatta, ne?
good, right?

and my dad emails
wow!

and I think
yeah
to all three

I post some photos
for friends
then separately
email them to Lisa

Chapter 25
Send-off

When Obon is over and
Kota has left and
we've taken down
the inside altar
and Koichi and I are taking down
the birdhouse altar
I murmur something like
until next year
but Koichi says *no*
don't say that

it seems the birdhouse altar
is used only for funerals
and the three Obon seasons
after a death
but never
when there is
not a death
in the family

now I remember thinking the altar
was a garden decoration
during that week we were here
for Jiichan's funeral
and now I understand
why Baachan comes outside
to watch as Koichi and I
remove the greenery and
dismantle the wood sections
and now I know why
she sighs so
heavy

three years
since Jiichan's death
over

he has truly
left us

if I were in New York
I would do like my Jewish cousins
with their relatives and
drape an arm over her shoulders
or take her hand
or give her a hug
but Kohama is not New York
and Baachan is not Jewish
and Baachan never
ever
hugs

she grunts
and fusses
and tells us to put the used greenery in the truck
and sweep the garden clean
where the altar stood
even though we know
and had already
started to do
just that

we resume work in the groves
thinning again the same groves
we were thinning in June
when I first arrived in Kohama

second pass
Uncle says
makes for sweeter fruit
less stress on the trees

so now we thin to get rid of
inferior fruit
scarred fruit
animal-damaged or
punctured fruit
any fruit unsuitable for market

but it seems a waste
so much good fruit
just tossed to the ground
so at the end of one day I ignore
Uncle's frown
and gather *mikan*
that aren't rotten
or split
or drilled with beak holes
into a bin

after the dinner dishes
and under Baachan's scowl
I squeeze the hard green fruits
juicing till my wrist and forearm ache

then add sugar
more
and more
and more sugar
far more sugar than Baachan wants to spare
for a drink
of discarded *mikan*

but when I stir and pour
a glass for her
with ice cubes
even she admits
it's better than lemonade

I take tiny glassfuls
to the others
and even set one
at the altar
for the ancestors

and you, too, Ruth,
if you'd like
a sip

Chapter 26
Friend

After thinning in the groves
all day one day
I come in from work
and on the table by the phone
lies a letter for me

not from my mother
or father
or Emi
but from Jake

friend I say to Baachan
whose eyebrows are way up and
who I know
wants to know
who it's from

she doesn't say so but
later I know
she will also
want to know
what it says

after my bath
sitting on my futon
I read Jake's words
on a half page of notebook paper

words that
stay with me
play over and over
in my head
even after *Physics and You*
even after Newton's prisms
even long after Yurie has turned off
the light

it's good to know someone cares
I keep wishing I'd done more
like we do for my sister
even though that's no guarantee
she won't do what Ruth did
someday

I try not to hate Lisa
for what she did
but it's hard
I try not to hate myself, too
I try not to hate all of us
for what we didn't do

lying there
in the dark
I wonder if Jake's list
of what we didn't do
is the same as my list
which is

      end the texting
      talk with you
      laugh with you
      listen to you
      include you

which seems so
basic and short
I keep thinking
there must be
something
else

in the morning Baachan
still has those eyebrows
way up
gives me extra work
shadows me
won't let me go to the groves
keeps me with her
on the roof hanging laundry
in the gardens watering
on an errand to the tofu shop
like my very first days
in Kohama

she doesn't ask
about the *friend* who wrote
doesn't talk
about Jake's letter
doesn't mention it
all morning
but finally
as I rinse the rice for lunch
I tell her
who it's from
and what it says

Baachan nods
and grunts
and mutters
and we eat lunch
and I go up to the groves
but when I come back down
end of the day
she says

shouldn't you
maybe consider
telling this Jake boy
to write
to that girl,
Lisa?

that night I check email
and with still no reply from Lisa
about my photos
I decide to do
what Baachan suggests—
write another letter to Jake
and tell him how quiet
Lisa has been
online

how I know she feels bad
how I think words
from him
might help

I start to write it out on paper
then turn on the computer
and this time
I send it by
email

then wait

okay
he emails back
in the morning, his night

nothing else

Chapter 27
Postcard

Mid-August
is the regular
Obon holiday
with most of Japan
off work and even Yurie
home two days
midweek

Uncle and Aunt keep working
saying
they've had their summer break
Kohama Obon

but Koichi and Yurie and I
are free to play

so we put mats, snorkels, masks, towels
and three of Baachan's *bento* lunches
in Koichi's car
blast music as we drive
down the west coast of the peninsula
curve after curve
of cliff
high above the sea

Yurie puts her hands in the air
and sways to the music
and the curves

I've never seen her
this way
relaxed
fun
acting young

we arrive at a crescent beach
edged by a village
of yellow and blue and red roofs
and backed by mountains
and flanked by craggy bluffs
on both sides

I think
I might just stay here forever

we change
then drop our bags onto
mats we set on the sand
and Koichi points to a float
takes his mark like the start of a race
says *yoi . . . ∂on!*
and we three fly to the water
charge
        splash forward
                dive under
                        swim crawl
hard as we can
out to the float

we climb up
rub our eyes
catch our breath
but not for long . . .

Koichi shoves us off
dives over us
and when we come up for air
says
race!
and we
swim the crawl hard
back to shore

later he hands us masks and snorkels
leads us down the beach
to where there are rocks offshore
we fit our masks
adjust our snorkels
start to swim
but Koichi stops
yells
then Yurie stops
yells
then I stop
yell
as we are stung
by jellyfish
and we *race!*
for real
back to shore

at the first-aid tent they say
the jellyfish are early this year
we rub ointment
on our stings
return to our mats
and after eating
Baachan's *bento* lunches
of all five proper colors
we make sand castles
with moats and turrets
and tunnels
and shell windows
then I treat us all
to heaping bowls of shaved ice
with sweet
azuki

I would have stayed here forever
if not
for the jellyfish
I say
and Yurie says
as she lies back on a mat
and closes her eyes
she might stay forever
anyway

while they doze
I go up to the shops
behind the seawall
and buy postcards

old discolored cards
with shots from different villages
showing Mount Fuji in a different
season with snow on its peak

I address one to Emi anyhow
but instead of words
I draw a picture:
crescent beach
mountains
bluffs
village roofs
me with ballooning shorts
          over my big butt
Koichi and Yurie
          stick figures
sand castle
water
waves
float

          and a mammoth jellyfish offshore

Chapter 28
Heat

The *mikan*
that we continue to thin
are large as baseballs
in some groves
enough to roll an ankle
if you step wrong
and if you step right
enough to make a juicy mess

tree after tree
row after row
terrace after terrace
we thin

I ask when the fruits
will finally
turn orange
September
they say
soon after you leave

and I'm disappointed
having wanted to see
row after row
terrace after terrace
of orange-spotted trees

the heat is brutal
making us slow and dull
as cicadas whine, drone and click
and do their crazy calls
so loud sometimes
we have to yell
to each other

we take extra water in thermoses
extra breaks in the shade
and after lunch
don't ever go back up
till after two
when the sun is starting
its slow track down
toward the western
horizon

which means
every day
after lunch cleanup
at the house
I have a full hour free
in Yurie's room
to nap or email
even chat online
with friends up late
in New York

and to the old atom of friends
humor
starts to return

barely noticeable
at first
like a tide change

summer will end soon
then high school —
private for Erin and Abby
public for the rest of us
bigger school
more activities
more options
more atoms

we make plans
to meet for pizza
the day before classes
the day before the start
of our next four years

and we joke about
what we'll bring each other
as gifts —

moose turds
rocks
math books
jellyfish salad

I send a separate email to Lisa
still quiet
and ask

how are you?
how's summer school?
ready for more school?

and she replies
right away

k
btw, jake emailed

I tell this to Baachan
and all afternoon in the hot groves
cutting the no-good fruit down
and pruning twigs
that will scar the rinds
I think
how cool is that

that what
Baachan said
to me
over here
made that
Jake-and-Lisa contact
happen
over there

at night
I think
there must be a way
to go beyond who we were
when what you did froze
the way we were
in everyone's heads

I think there must be a way
to show you
we've grown
and to show you
that maybe now
we know how
we should have been
with you, Ruth,

and that maybe
now we'd know
how to keep you
from walking
up that hill
that night
to the orchard
behind Jake's house

Chapter 29
Different

One day we come down
from the groves for lunch
hot, beat
drenched in sweat
but before I finish my second glass
of cold barley tea
Baachan sends me out
to buy tofu

when I return she hovers
says Yurie called to tell me
the computer
isn't working

all through lunch she repeats
Yurie said don't touch it!
don't even turn it on!

which is weird
because I was the last one to use it
when Yurie went to bed last night
and neither of us had it on
this morning

Koichi is off for the day
dealing with some truck repair
so Baachan tells me to take my after-lunch break
with Uncle on the veranda
and he'll teach me how to play *shogi*
I sit down opposite my uncle
thinking this is different—
he always naps
in this heat

Uncle sets up the board
starts explaining the sides
sente and *gote*
the moves of the king
the gold and silver generals
chariots
knights and dragon horses
and I'm thinking
enough already
let's play

but the phone rings
Baachan answers
and Aunt hovers
like she caught it from Baachan
and Baachan hands the phone to Aunt
and Aunt disappears into the kitchen
and Baachan orders us
to stop *shogi* immediately
and sends Uncle and me
on an errand to get some . . .

cucumbers?
Uncle and me?
Uncle never does the vegetable picking and
Baachan never wastes two bodies
on a task that
could be done
by one

but we get the cucumbers
though Baachan didn't say how many
and some peppers and
eggplants to be safe
but it is way too hot in the gardens
mid-August
midday

we start to walk back
but Uncle gets a call on his cell
says a few words
then ends the call
looks at me

and tells me he needs to talk
with his cousin who runs
the gas station

so we go
all the way there
opposite side of the village
and it's so hot I'm wishing
I had one of Baachan's
big
ugly
bonnets

Uncle and gas station man
talk and talk
as I sip cold tea
and watch gas station man's
wife put gas
in cars
air in tires
wash windshields
make change

between customers she sits with me
tells me about her grown kids
learning to drive

but on the way home
Uncle remembers he forgot
the cucumbers
I have only eggplants and peppers
and he insists we both
return to the gas station
and I'm thinking
this is different

Uncle never wastes an afternoon
and never visits during work hours
and normally doesn't care
about cucumbers or if he did
would go back himself
and send me ahead
to help Baachan
or Aunt
with a chore

even after
we get the cucumbers
he remembers
suddenly
sheepishly
we need to see another cousin
by the bridge

but by then I'm thinking
this is way too
different

and I start to run

through the east side
of the village
over the bridge
to the west side
down the lane
up the driveway
through the house
past Baachan and Aunt
in the kitchen
up to Yurie's room
where I let the
eggplants and peppers
drop

Uncle
not far behind me
is hollering through the house
as I'm kneeling before the computer
cursing it to boot up
           fast
                     faster
                               damn it!

Baachan flies into the room
tries to pull me away
Uncle behind her
Aunt, too
but Uncle pulls Baachan off me
and I look at Baachan
see her eyes fill and
I know

something
happened

please
I say

Chapter 30
News

Baachan kneels beside me then
before the low table with the computer
that she doesn't know how to use
as I open the browser
and pull up my email
and chat
and see all the
messages
and the name
again
and again

Lisa

Baachan holds me
as I check each message
first from Lisa to us all
last night, Japan night
her morning
just an hour after I
logged off

thanks everyone
you've been great but it's
time to go
gotta make myself
better
only way
I know how
luv you
Lisa

then message after message
copied to every electron
in the atom
and beyond
as they logged on
then phoned
and emailed
anyone
everyone
desperate
to get someone
at the summer school
to find her
stop her
save her

and messages
hours later
after they got the news
from their mothers
who'd heard from Abby's mother
who'd heard direct
from Lisa's godmother
that she'd been found

in her dorm room
hanging
from her bathrobe sash

Baachan says
that a phone call before breakfast
was my mother with the news
and that my mother
wanted me to hear the news from her
not a computer

but that she had to comfort Emi
take Emi to meet with counselors
that Gina's father had assembled
at the community center
for girls, siblings, friends, parents
anyone in town
who needed help . . .
so could they stall?

my mother had thought
they'd be home to call
during our lunch break
but they were delayed
as more and more girls, boys
parents and neighbors arrived

so my mother had called my father
who'd called here
during *shogi* and told Baachan
stall more!

now Aunt brings the phone upstairs
and they dial my home
in New York

I hear my mother's words
I hear her voice
and my dad comes on
and I hear his words
hear his voice
all soft
and Emi comes on
and I hear her words
and I hear her voice

but I have none

and Aunt takes the phone
then gives it to Uncle
who leaves the room

I start to shiver
my whole body
and Aunt sets out the futon
and Baachan lays me down
and Aunt covers me
and Yurie comes home from work early
and stays beside me
lies beside me
holds me

at night I wake
in the dark
and turn
and Baachan
on a futon beside mine
turns toward me
pats my back
and Yurie on her futon
beside mine
turns toward me
takes my hand

somehow I sleep
between them
all night

Chapter 31
Body A, Body B

I lie there
a doctor comes
I take a pill
and sleep
wake
sleep
soups are brought
I sip
sleep

when I wake
someone is always there
someone always takes my hand
strokes my head

I don't eat till late
the next day
almost dark
again
when Baachan
brings me a plate
of pancakes
covered with canned slices of *mikan*
and sweet whipped cream
which she spears mouthfuls of
on a fork
and feeds me
as I tremble
and stop
to cry

when I can finally speak
to my mother
by phone
I learn that
as it turns out
in Lisa's pocket
was a printout
of an email
from Jake

who wrote

we can't hate ourselves
just find a way to make this
turn you into someone
better than you were
that's what we all have to do
that's all we can do

I translate this to Baachan
who squeezes her eyes shut
shakes her head
mournful, slow

and uses that handkerchief
that's always tucked and ready
in her front
apron pocket

Newton's third law
of reciprocal action
says
for every action there is an equal
and opposite
reaction
that all forces are interactions
all forces come in pairs

Physics and You
spells it out
says
if body A exerts a force
on body B
then body B will exert a force
of the same magnitude
on body A

push and pull

I think
maybe this
is what happened
with Lisa
and you, Ruth—
body A
and body B

Chapter 32
Mistakes

After two and a half days
Baachan tells me to get up
and shower
and then come help
in the kitchen

start your body moving she says
your mind will follow

Yurie has left for work
Aunt, Uncle and Koichi are in the groves
they've all eaten
Baachan's washing up
I sit at the table alone

I eat rice, miso soup
then Baachan and I
go for a walk
up to the temple

before the heat starts
before the cicadas
are deafening
when there is still
coolness to be found
in shade

we trudge uphill
Baachan pausing often
to wipe her brow and neck
with her handkerchief
as we climb higher
beyond the temple
up terraces
of stone monuments

we bow before the Mano grave
Baachan standing in prayer
long after I have opened my eyes
to stare at family names

at the temple
closed and quiet
we ascend stone steps
and sit down
on the weathered boards
of the veranda
under the deep eave
facing the bay
and faint gray hint
of Mount Fuji

suicide can spread
Baachan finally says
utsuru she adds
like a virus

you have to stop it
put up barriers

I rock back and forth
exhale
ask

do you think it was a mistake —
the letter to Jake
the email from Jake
to Lisa?

a hot wind gusts
behind us
from the south
curling over the mountaintop
brushing tree canopies
and rolling down the slopes
to breathe on us like dragon fire
there
on the veranda

no she says
what I think was a mistake
was sending a girl
of fourteen away
to a different state
to live in a dormitory
by herself
during a summer like this

meaning a summer
after what you did
with the rope
in Osgoods' orchard

I say to Baachan
but I was sent away, too
to another country
far from home

and Baachan looks at me
like I'm truly twisted
says
far from home?
what are you saying?
you came home, Kana-chan,
you came home to family

Chapter 33
Surprise

That afternoon
I start work again
in the groves
thinning
and solving problems
with Koichi
in the mountain air
above the bay

and some *mikan*
in the lowest groves
are just turning color
the stubborn green
finally going yellow

we take a day off
during my last week
all six of us
and drive the van
up the Shonan coast
to Kamakura
to visit the
Big Buddha
where I light incense
and for once
know what to say
when I pray

which is for you
and Lisa both
to find peace

then two days before
my flight home
there is a surprise

a farewell dinner
for me
at Asuka's house

sliding doors have been removed
in several rooms
to make a long hall
for two rows
of low tables
with men down the farthest ends
and women toward the entrance
sitting and rising and going
back and forth and
in and out of the kitchen

there are heaps of food
and bottles of drinks
brought by cousins
and second cousins
and aunts and uncles
and people from the village
and a few from beyond
and Asuka and Rika and Ai
and even a few girls
from my class at the
middle school
everyone spilling out into
side rooms
the entryway
the driveway even

on cue from Yurie
I take bottles
of beer and sake and
oolong tea and juice
and go from person to person
pouring into their glasses
speaking my thanks
bowing
smiling
chatting
whether I remember
who
they are
or not

and they start to talk
about my mother
and my father
and someone says that
it is time for them
to visit
and someone else says
that a party with them
would be good
but I mention that
with my mother's business
winter is better
since it's difficult
for her to leave in summer

and suddenly they ask
if I will be back
next summer

I bow
and say
if they will have me

then add
and if they will have Emi, too

some handkerchiefs come out
and there are cheers
and Asuka and Rika and Ai rush
to pour more drinks

and then the men
joke that Uncle's fall harvest
will be bigger next year
with all that extra summer help
that they will have to work hard
to keep up and will have to see
what relatives they can get
to come help, too

Chapter 34
Crumbs

Then I'm back
in New York
in my room with Emi
talking about the groves
and missing the scent
of *mikan* on my hands
wishing I could have stayed
a few more weeks
for the start of the fall harvest
just to see those mountain slopes
with row after terraced row of trees
with *mikan* all turned orange

the day after I arrive
I go see Jake
riding my bike up
the hill you climbed
alone that night

his mom hugs me
in the driveway
then shakes her head
and gives me a deep look
and I know
he's been having a hard time

he and I
sit on wicker chairs
on their porch
but neither of us
speaks

can we walk? I finally ask

he nods
and we go down the steps

after we've walked
away from their house
along the road that continues uphill
and that has hardly any traffic
ever

I stop on the rough edge of the asphalt
turn to him and am about to say
that I'm sorry and more
but Jake warns
don't

he glares then looks off, way off
to where the road dips
and beyond where a hill rises
to a wooded dome

he eyes me
his look hard, steely
then softer
pained

can I ask a favor? I finally ask

he waits, suspicious
and I almost don't ask
but I do

the tree . . .
can I see it?

he seems to inflate with anger
and I think he's going to send me away
as he exhales and inhales
like a squall

I wait
for the weather in his eyes
to shift

when it finally does
he leads me back down the road
up their driveway
behind their house
and into the orchard

we walk down
the central rutted road
ahead of me Jake
dragging his feet
kicking up dust

when he turns left into a row
I pause
follow again
and stop when he stops
at the third tree

he exhales
then raises his arm
and points upward

I follow with my eyes
and can't help
but cry out

because somehow, Ruth,
I'd pictured
a branch still
spring-bare
and nearly empty
but the branch
Jake points to
is full
heavy
drooping with
the most stunning
abundance
of ripe apples

Jake and I sit down beneath
that abundance and
for a long time we don't talk

when I do finally speak
I tell Jake that
later this month
we will visit
our cousins for Rosh Hashanah
and join the Tashlich walk
along the river
as we do each year

to focus on the past year
casting crumbs of bread
symbolizing our sins, our mistakes
into the water

and I say I will have to cast a whole
loaf of bread
or several
to equal enough crumbs
for all my mistakes
this past year

he nods
then says
I'd need a loaf, too

no, I say
not you
there's just one important crumb
you need to cast

which one's that? he asks

and I say
the one for blaming yourself

Chapter 35
Pact

Two days later is
the memorial service
for Lisa, delayed so all of us
who've been away can attend
and where your mother
gives a moving speech to us all
has us hold hands, Ruth,
until everyone in the chapel
is connected
in one big
tangled chain

she begs us
each link
in that community chain
to make a pact to do
what you can't do
what Lisa can't do
anymore —

which is
live

then when she speaks of her idea to create
a memorial among some trees
in a section of orchard
that Jake's family has offered to
donate

I start
        thinking
        seeing
        sketching
in my head

as the service goes on
tearful speeches one after another
tributes to Lisa
pleas to us all
it is like
I am drawing in the dirt
in the *mikan* groves
with Koichi

later I tell
Emi
my mother
my father
and they tell me to draw
in earnest
and take me to an art store
for supplies

and then I do a difficult thing
which is to call
your mother
to tell her
my idea

she invites me to come
to your house the next week
after school

and there
in your dining room
your dogs checking me out
I unroll and show her
my plan

which is
for a path
of flat stones
that meanders
through the orchard
one stone to represent
each of us former
eighth-grade girls

stones leading to a gazebo
with benches for
sitting
talking
watching the trees
the rhythm of the year
in sap, leaves, buds, fruit

the cycle of growth and rest
growth and rest

I tell her that
every year when the
apples are in blossom
we'll gather
decorate the gazebo
with new greens
bring you and Lisa
your favorite foods
and light small welcome fires
for you both
to join us

and maybe we'll sing
or play some music
maybe we'll dance
or at least walk
around the gazebo
and maybe we'll picnic
in the orchard
or maybe not

but definitely we'll share
our hopes
dreams
goals
all the ways we promise
to survive
another year
without you both

your mother
nods
and starts to move her mouth

but then she furrows her brow
and says
just one thing —

can you make
those stepping stones enough
for all the eighth-grade girls
and boys?

I say
of course
not knowing why
I didn't think of that myself

then I wait

as your mother studies my drawings
leans over them
runs her fingers over my
careful pen lines and letters

and underneath
the dogs sigh and
settle down
at my feet

she sits up straight
breathes in deep
with effort it seems

yes
she finally says

she would be pleased
if I shared the plan with
Jake and his family
and if they approve
and your father and brother approve
and if Lisa's godparents approve
she would be especially pleased
if I made the design
and built the memorial
with everyone's help

as I leave your house
to bike home
I am bursting with
ideas
pedaling madly
nearly going off
the side of the road
into a ditch

I find my mother in the field
tending her Japanese pumpkins
and I share the news

later I call Jake
who comes over to check the plans
no, scrutinize the plans
and make suggestions

and when we get the go-ahead
I call Ken
and Abby and Emily
and Gina
and Namita
who all agree to help
with the construction
if I will tell them
what to do

I don't tell them that first
I have to learn
myself
what to do

I call others
every single one
of last year's eighth-grade girls
and boys

and very last I call Noah
who I'd forgotten
I had a crush on
way back
in the months
that seem like
ages ago
before all this happened

Noah, who I have not even
thought of once
in that way
since you walked up the hill
to Osgoods' orchard
that night

just looking at him
used to be hard for me
talking to him
unthinkable

but now I just call
start speaking
right away

and he, too
says sure,
he'll help

so I start the plans
for real

I visit
lumberyards
hardware stores
garden centers
websites
libraries
stonecutters
and even sign up for
a continuing-ed carpentry course
at the community college

knowing that
next spring we'll gather for you
and Lisa
meet with you
feed your spirits

and afterward
we'll say farewell
for a year

and we'll
go on

Acknowledgments

My deepest gratitude to all my *mikan* farming friends in the Nishiura district of Numazu City, Shizuoka Prefecture, most especially Hiroshi Arai and family, who welcomed me into their groves for eighteen months to learn every aspect of *mikan* cultivation, from planting to harvest. Enormous thanks also to Ellen Hopkins and Suzanne Morgan Williams for the Nevada SCBWI Mentor Program and to my amazing mentor, Esther Hershenhorn; to Gerda Klein and Randi Klein, for their patient guidance; to my careful readers Adam Clark, Asako Clark, Laura Shovan and Avery Udagawa; to all my SCBWI Tokyo writer and illustrator friends; to my agent, Jamie Weiss Chilton; and to my editor, Françoise Bui. And thanks always and forever to Bob, Dexter and Isabel — you keep me going.

About the Author

HOLLY THOMPSON grew up in New England. She earned a BA in biology from Mount Holyoke College and an MA in English with a concentration in creative writing from New York University. A longtime resident of Japan, she teaches creative and academic writing at Yokohama City University. Her stories and articles have been published in magazines in the United States and Japan, and she is the author of the novel *Ash* and the picture book *The Wakame Gatherers*. Visit her online at hatbooks.com.

8/10/11